EILEEN SPINELLI

Lizzie Logan, Second Banana

ALADDIN PAPERBACKS

New York   London   Toronto   Sydney   Singapore

First Aladdin Paperbacks edition January 2000

Copyright © 1998 by Eileen Spinelli

Aladdin Paperbacks
An imprint of Simon & Schuster Children's Publishing Division
1230 Avenue of the Americas
New York, NY 10020

All rights reserved, including the right of reproduction
in whole or in part in any form.

The text for this book was set in 14-point Zapf Calligraphic.
Printed and bound in the United States of America.
2 4 6 8 10 9 7 5 3

The Library of Congress has cataloged the hardcover edition as follows:
Spinelli, Eileen.
Lizzie Logan, second banana / Eileen Spinelli.
p. cm.
Summary: When Lizzie's mother announces that she is gong to have a baby,
her best friend Heather helps her deal with her fears that her stepfather
will love the new baby more than her.
ISBN 0-689-81510-7 (hc.)
[1. Babies—Fiction. 2. Stepfathers—Fiction. 3. Best friends—Fiction.] I. Title.
PZ7.S7566Lh 1998
[E]-dc21
97-23905
ISBN 0-689-83048-3 (Aladdin pbk.)

To Linda Francis, Alice Smith, Marie Monkiewicz, and Judy Anderson . . .
hello forever!
—E. S.

Contents

1. Pickwick — 1
2. Whistling — 6
3. Frogs Don't Drink Water — 10
4. A Surprise in the Mudroom — 15
5. Moon Girls — 19
6. Not a Beauty Contest — 23
7. Spies — 27
8. Michigan — 31
9. Garfish and Cigar Sharks — 34
10. Baby-sitting the Woolery Twins — 39
11. Marigold Seeds — 43
12. No More Lizzie Logan — 46
13. Good-bye, Winter — 51
14. Second Banana — 55
15. Almost April — 59
16. No Turning Back — 62
17. Five Contestants — 66
18. And the Winner Is — 70
19. Worried — 72
20. Here's What Happened — 78
21. Hello — 82

1
Pickwick

It was the middle of February. A cold, dreary Saturday. I was putting a puzzle together at the kitchen table. Mom was in the basement doing laundry.

Suddenly she screamed.

I ran down the steps. I found her slumped against the washing machine. Her face was white as chalk.

"Mom!" I cried. "Are you okay?"

She pointed to the washer. "I did a terrible thing."

Mom had done terrible things to the wash before. Once she'd mixed a red shirt with Dad's underwear, and everything turned pink.

I figured she had done that again. I patted her arm. "Don't worry," I told her. "Dad is used to having pink underwear."

A tear rolled down my mother's cheek. "It's not Dad's underwear."

"His pajamas?"

Mom shook her head. "No."

"*My* pajamas?"

"I wish." Mom sniffled. "It's . . . it's . . . Pickwick."

"Pickwick!" I shrieked. "You stuck *Pickwick* in the *washing* machine?"

"I thought he needed a bath."

My heart thumping, I inched closer to the washer. I peered in. There was Pickwick, my beloved teddy bear.

Uncle Frank had given me Pickwick for my third birthday. I'd cuddled up with him every night for five years. Only this wasn't Pickwick anymore. This was a few ragged swatches of furry material. A soppy ball of stuffing. Two black buttons.

I plopped to the floor. Mom plopped down next to me and pulled me close. She kissed the top of my head. "I'll make it up to you, sweetie."

We gave Dad the job of removing Pickwick's remains. I watched from the window as he plunked Pickwick into the trash can. "Good-bye, old pal," I sobbed. "Good-bye."

Later I called my best friend, Lizzie Logan.

"Pickwick's dead." I sniffled.

"Huh?"

"Mom washed him to death."

Lizzie sighed. "Heather, you are one lucky dude."

I screeched. "Lucky? Didn't you hear me? Pickwick is dead."

"I heard you." Her voice was calm and cool.

"Well, thanks for the sympathy."

"Look," she said, "you're too old for teddy bears anyway."

"Says you."

"Right, says me. And now your mom's gonna feel rotten for at least a week."

"So?"

"So you have your mom right where you want her. For at least a week you can have anything you want. Maybe two weeks."

"I can?"

"Listen, what's for dinner tonight?"

"Macaroni and cheese, I think."

"Fine. Tell your mom you're not in the mood for macaroni and cheese."

"She'll just tell me to eat a little."

"Not tonight she won't."

"She won't?"

"Trust me. Tell her tonight you're in the mood for chocolate ice cream."

I had to laugh. "Lizzie, my mother is not gonna let me eat chocolate ice cream for supper."

Lizzie's voice got smooth as hot fudge. "*Tonight* she will."

• • •

It was dinnertime. Mom was smiling softly. "How much macaroni and cheese would you like, Heather?"

I thought about what Lizzie had told me. I decided to test it out. I cleared my throat. "Uh, I'm not in the mood for macaroni and cheese tonight."

Mom put the serving spoon down. She gave me a sad look. "I understand, sweetie."

I plowed on. "I just feel like eating ice cream tonight. Chocolate."

Mom nodded. Then she tweaked Dad's cheek. "George, dear, can you run down to Martin's Market for some ice cream?"

Dad tossed his napkin on the table. "Sure thing, hon."

I could almost see Lizzie grinning like a toothpaste commercial.

The truth is, though, that night when Dad came back with a half gallon of Dutch fudge chocolate, I wasn't in the mood for that either.

2
Whistling

The following week it was Lizzie's turn for troubles.

She was in her backyard wearing an old hard hat and floppy rain boots. She was digging a hole.

Lizzie digs holes when she's upset.

It started in December when her dog, Charley, got hit by a car. They had to take him to the vet. Lizzie was scared that Charley might not make it. She said she felt like her heart was a brick, and that digging holes made her feel better.

Luckily, Charley recovered. But the hole digging stuck.

Hole digging didn't work for me.

I tried it a couple of days after Mom drowned Pickwick. I dug near the back fence. I dug up Mom's daffodil bulbs. By mistake, of course. Mom didn't even fuss at me. But no matter how deep I dug, I still missed Pickwick.

Now I touched Lizzie's arm. "What's the matter?" I asked.

Lizzie stopped digging to give me a sour ball look. "Mom's going to have a baby. In August."

This was *good* news. "That's super!" I said.

"It's goosepoop," she snarled.

"Goosepoop?"

"You heard me."

"What, you don't want a baby brother or sister?"

"Nope."

"Why not?"

"Because I already have Charley."

"But Charley's a dog!"

"Right. Two parents. One kid. One dog. The perfect family."

Lizzie's family hadn't always been so perfect.

Lizzie's father, Mr. Logan, had left when

she was a baby. She never heard from him again. That made Lizzie sad.

Then, this past November, Lizzie's mom married Sam Bright, a guy who makes the world's best pancakes. Lizzie finally had what she always wanted: a dad at home.

Lizzie tossed another shovelful of dirt. "You know what the worst part is?"

"What?"

"The whistling."

"Huh?"

"The whistling. Dad never stops. He whistles in the morning over the frying pan. He whistles coming through the door after work." She snorted. "He even whistles in the bathroom."

I love hearing her call Sam "Dad." She made the switch the instant he married her mother, and she hasn't called him Sam since.

"I guess he's just happy," I said.

Lizzie poked the air with her finger. "Exactly!"

I flashed her a look. "Don't you want Sam to be happy?"

"Of course I do, noodlehead. I want him to be happy about *me*."

"He is." I reminded Lizzie of her parents' wedding day. "Remember how he hugged you? Kissed you? Even cried?"

"Yeah." Lizzie smirked. "But did he *whistle*?"

3
Frogs Don't Drink Water

Lizzie's mom stuck her head out the back door. She was eating a beef stick.

"Hi, Mrs. Bright," I said. I still felt strange calling the former Mrs. Logan "Mrs. Bright." But she was married to Sam now and she had Sam's last name.

Someday Lizzie would have Sam's last name, too, after a bunch of legal stuff was done. For now, she was still Lizzie Logan.

Mrs. Bright waved. "Hi, Heather."

"Congratulations!" I said.

She grinned. "Lizzie told you our news?"

"Yep."

"Goosepoop," Lizzie muttered under her breath.

"Time to put the shovel away, Lizzie," said Mrs. Bright. "Your dentist appointment's in one hour."

Lizzie looked at her rain forest watch. "Double goosepoop."

I patted Lizzie's shoulder. "See ya later, gator."

Back home I found Mom in the kitchen. She was rinsing a piece of old lace in the sink. She and Dad and Uncle Frank are partners in an antique shop called The Good Old Days. That's where the lace was headed.

I nudged Mom with my elbow. "Guess what I just heard?"

She dried her hands on a dish towel. "What?"

"Lizzie's mom is going to have a baby."

"I know."

I screeched. "No fair! Grown-ups know everything first."

"Sorry, sweetie."

I pouted my way through five chocolate chip cookies. Mom didn't try to stop me.

Then I went off to do my homework, a report on frogs.

I found some facts in the encyclopedia. For example, most frogs lay their eggs in water. And the female frog is usually bigger than the male. But my teacher, Miss Kelsey, says encyclopedia facts alone make for a boring paper. I decided to wait until Lizzie got back from the dentist, then I'd check out frogs with her.

I'm in third grade. Lizzie's in fifth. That makes her two years smarter than me. And that's not all. Lizzie watches oodles of public television—oodles of it—and she reads all the time. So I think she might be smarter than anyone, except maybe the president.

• • •

"Frogs?" said Lizzie that evening as I plopped into her purple beanbag chair. "I can tell you lots. Frogs have teeth. Did you know that?"

I patted Charley, who was trying to climb into my lap. "No, I didn't know that."

"And frogs don't drink water."

I gaped at her. "Don't they get thirsty?"

"Sure they do, noodlehead."

"So how come they don't drink water?"

Lizzie clamped her hands on her hips. "Because they *absorb* it. Right through their skin."

Lizzie also told me that a frog can't swallow unless it closes its eyes. "And once," she said, "it *rained* frogs in Russia."

Miss Kelsey couldn't say *that* was boring!

When Lizzie was finally frogged out, we went downstairs for ice cream. Charley came, too.

Lizzie's mom was sitting on the sofa eating a beef stick and watching the news. She smiled as we passed.

In the kitchen Lizzie gave Charley a dog treat. Then we each filled a bowl with vanilla ice cream. I drenched mine in chocolate syrup. Lizzie spooned peanut butter on hers.

Back in the living room, the news was still on. A local newscaster announced that The Bagel Box was closing. "Too bad," said Lizzie's mom. "They had the best bagels."

Charley barked. "Even Charley thinks so," said Mrs. Bright.

But Charley wasn't barking about bagels. He had heard something. Lizzie and I heard it, too. It was whistling. Faint at first. Then louder and louder as the whistler moved nearer to the house.

The front door opened. Sam whistled in.

Lizzie poked me in the ribs. I turned. She was wearing her fiercest "I-told-you-so" look.

4
A Surprise in the Mudroom

After school the next day Lizzie suggested we go to The Bagel Box.

"What for?" I asked.

"To say good-bye, jelly brain. It's closing."

At The Bagel Box Mrs. Findley, the owner, was packing up.

"We came to pay our condolences," Lizzie said, all grown-up like.

I whispered, "Who died?"

Lizzie hissed, "No one, dummy."

Mrs. Findley handed each of us a blueberry bagel. Free. "It was sweet of you girls to stop by," she said.

Lizzie patted Mrs. Findley's arm. "We'll miss you."

I felt I should say something, too, something cheery. "At least nobody died."

Lizzie kicked me in the ankle and said, "So who bought the place?"

Mrs. Findley sighed. "Granny Fryola. She's putting in a fish store."

As we left we bumped into Mrs. Woolery and her three-year-old twins, Betsy and Bootsie. I pointed to The Bagel Box. "Joey Fryola's grandmother bought it," I said. "It's going to be a fish store."

Betsy pinched her nose. "Ewww. Fish stink."

Bootsie nodded. "Stink. Stink. Stink."

"Stink!" said Betsy.

"Stink! Stink!" said Bootsie.

"That's enough!" snapped Mrs. Woolery.

When the Woolerys were gone, I grinned at Lizzie. "Maybe your mom will have twins."

Lizzie bonked me over the head with her bagel.

• • •

When I got home Uncle Frank was in the living room looking pleased about something. He tweaked my nose. "How's my short-stuff?"

"Fine," I said, taking off my coat. "I got an A on my frog report."

"Way to go!" He danced me around the coffee table.

Mom appeared. "Did you tell her about the surprise?"

I looked up at Uncle Frank. "What surprise? Where?"

Uncle Frank's face dimpled into a grin. "In the mudroom."

Mom beamed. "Wait till you see."

I hoped it wasn't a new teddy bear. No one could replace Pickwick.

I went back to the mudroom. The surprise was not a teddy bear at all. It was a telescope. A *real* telescope. Brand-new. Black. Shiny.

"Like it?" said Uncle Frank.

I hugged him so hard, the two of us nearly fell into the laundry basket.

I had asked for a telescope for Christmas, but sales at The Good Old Days weren't so good this winter. Dad said maybe for my birthday, in April. Now, here it was only February. I could hardly believe my eyes.

I couldn't wait until dark. I couldn't wait to see the stars.

Uncle Frank said we might not be able to see many. We live too near the city, and so there was too much light in the sky. But we'd see some. And the moon, too. "And someday," he said, "we'll go to a star party. At Valley Forge Park."

Uncle Frank had been telling me about star parties lately. They're magical, he says. No food. No music. No balloons. Only sky and stars and darkness and quiet.

"Can Lizzie come?" I said.

Uncle Frank nodded. "Absolutely."

I hugged him again.

5
Moon Girls

That night Lizzie helped me set up the telescope in my backyard.

She adjusted the barrel in and out.

"Let me see," I said.

"Hold your pants on!" she snapped.

It was cold. My breath came out all frosty. Lizzie was hunched over the eyepiece.

"What are you looking at?"

Lizzie barely whispered. "Moon."

"Give me a turn."

She stepped aside, grumbling.

I scrunched one eye shut and peered into the telescope with the other. I saw the moon. At first I was disappointed. "It's not all gold and shimmery," I said.

Lizzie sighed. "But, Heather, look how close it is. Like if we took three giant steps we'd be moon girls dancing across those craters."

It *was* an amazing picture. "Yeah!"

"You'd probably be impressed with Saturn," Lizzie told me. "Saturn has rings. Like Hula Hoops."

We looked and looked for Saturn, but could not find it.

Finally Dad called us in. "School tomorrow."

Lizzie folded up my telescope and carried it into the house. I could see she really liked it.

"Too bad you already had your birthday," I said. Lizzie had turned eleven on January sixteenth.

"Yeah," she replied. "I should have asked for a telescope."

"Instead of that Erupt-A-Volcano kit."

"Yeah," said Lizzie. "The stupid volcano never did blow up."

I pinched my nose. "It did smell, though."

Lizzie giggled. "Like rotten potatoes."

"Remember—your mom threw up?"

"Oh, that wasn't the volcano," said Lizzie. "That was morning sickness."

"Morning sickness?"

"Yeah. Mom didn't know it, but she was pregnant then."

"Being pregnant makes you throw up?"

"In the early stages. In the morning."

"Does your mom still throw up?"

"Nope."

"How come?"

"We found a cure."

"A cure?"

Lizzie nodded. "Beef sticks."

• • •

On the way to school the next day, Lizzie snarled. "Goosepoop! Goosepoop! Goosepoop!"

"Now what?" I said.

"My folks won't buy me a telescope."

"Never?"

"Not right now. Maybe my next birthday."

"Well," I said, "at least not never."

Lizzie gave me a poison ivy scowl. "*You* got one and it wasn't *your* birthday."

What could I say? It was true.

"And my folks bought the baby a new crib. And it's not the baby's birthday."

I rolled my eyes. "The baby has to have a place to sleep."

"Yeah, but does the baby *have* to have a dancing clown mobile? Huh? They bought that, too."

I shrugged.

"Will the baby croak if it doesn't go to sleep with stupid clowns dancing over its head?"

"Will *you* croak if you don't get a telescope?"

"People do die of broken hearts." Lizzie sniffed. "Just read the newspaper."

I had to laugh. "Lizzie Logan, are you saying your heart is broken just because you have to wait to get a telescope?"

"No." Lizzie sniffled. "Just because my parents love this poopy-doopy baby more than they love me!"

6
Not a Beauty Contest

By the end of February, Mom was over her guilt about Pickwick. Completely.

"I think I'm in the mood for French toast," I said one morning.

Mom had just cracked two eggs into a pan. "I'm making poached eggs," she said.

I nibbled on a slice of orange. "But I'm not in the mood for poached eggs."

Mom turned. She was wearing a goofy smile. "You're not?"

I leaned back in my chair. "Nope."

"That's funny. Yesterday you were in the mood for poached eggs."

"Yeah, but not today."

"Just not in the mood?"

"Not even a teensy-tinsey bit of a mood," I told her.

Five seconds later Mom was standing over me with a plate of eggs. "You've got two choices," she said.

"Huh?"

"You can *eat* these eggs, or you can *wear* these eggs. It's up to you."

I wailed, "MOOOOOOOMMMMMM!"

The plate tilted above my head. "Eat? Wear? What'll it be?"

She wasn't kidding. I gave a big sigh. "Eat," I grouched.

She set the plate in front of me and patted the top of my head. "Good girl."

• • •

March came and so did "The Little Miss Seafood Pageant" announcement.

Granny Fryola advertised it in the local newspaper. Girls between six and eleven could try out. The prize was a one hundred dollar bill and a box of crabcakes.

The winner would preside over the grand opening of Granny Fryola's Fish Store. She would be chosen for her costume, her smile, and her talent. The talent had to have something to do with fish, of course.

I wasn't surprised when Kayleen Bitterman was the first to sign up. Kayleen is in third grade, like me. On career day, when Miss Kelsey asked each of us to tell what we want to be when we grow up, Kayleen said, "Miss Universe."

I also wasn't surprised to learn that Sue-Ann LeBoon had signed up. Or Erica Chapko. They hang out with Kayleen and do whatever she does.

But when *Lizzie* told me *she* had entered, I nearly rolled off her beanbag chair.

We were in her room after school, eating pretzels. "You gotta be kidding!" I squealed.

"What's the matter?" she snapped. "Think I can't win?"

"But you hate beauty contests!"

"It's not a beauty contest, dummy. It's a costume-smile-and-talent contest. Besides, I want that one hundred dollar bill."

"I'd like a hundred dollar bill, too," I said. "But you don't see me trying to be Little Miss Seafood."

"That's because you already got your telescope."

"Boy, you want a telescope bad."

"Yeah, I do," she admitted. "That's why you have to help me win."

I gaped at her. "Me? How do I do that?"

"Easy." Lizzie crunched into a pretzel. "You become my manager."

7
Spies

A week later Lizzie and I were in my basement.

"Cover up the windows," Lizzie ordered.

"Why?"

"Just do it, noodlenose."

"Hey!" I said. "I thought I was the manager."

"You are."

"Then stop calling me noodlenose."

Lizzie glared at me. "I can call you noodlenose if it makes me happy. Part of your job is to make me happy."

"Oh, yeah? Then get somebody else."

"Okay," Lizzie said, "I will."

I put my hands on my hips. "Yeah, right." I smirked. "Who?"

Lizzie Logan was not the most popular kid on Mole Street.

"None of your beeswax."

Since she wasn't going to act mature, I figured it was up to me. "Look," I said, "be happy all you want. Just don't call me noodlenose."

"But I always call you noodlenose. It's a habit."

"You do not always call me noodlenose."

Lizzie nodded. "You're right. I call you noodle*head*, too."

I plopped down on an old lawn chair. "Just don't call me noodle anything. Not while I'm the manager."

"That's silly."

"It is not. The manager is the boss."

"Oh, no!" Lizzie cried. "I hired you. I'm the boss."

A truck rumbled up Mole Street. A door slammed in the distance. Finally Lizzie grumbled, "Okay. Okay. We'll both be the boss."

I guessed that was better than nothing.

"All right," I said. "We'll both be the boss."

We shook hands.

"Now," said Lizzie, "cover up those windows."

"Only if you tell me why."

Lizzie whistled through her teeth. "Christopher crabcakes, girl. Because of the spies."

"Spies on Mole Street?" I laughed.

"Go ahead," said Lizzie. "You won't be laughing when they steal my costume idea."

"Why would a government spy want to steal your costume idea?"

"Not a government spy, nood-uh-Heather," Lizzie said. "A spy for Kayleen Bitterman."

Lizzie's costume was going to be an octopus with arms made out of old vacuum cleaner hoses. Kayleen is a pink, lacy, paint-your-toenails kind of girl. I knew she wouldn't be caught dead wearing vacuum cleaner hoses.

I draped my arm around Lizzie. "You can stop worrying about Kayleen right now."

Lizzie pushed my arm away. Her face turned practically purple. She pointed to the window above the coal bin.

Betsy and Bootsie Woolery were there. Earmuff to earmuff. Noses pressed against the glass. Watching us. Grinning.

Lizzie yelped. "Spies!" She grabbed an old jacket from a cardboard box and climbed on top of the Christmas crates Mom kept in the coal bin. She draped the jacket across the window.

The Woolerys tapped on the glass. "Can we play, too?"

"See?" I said. "They just want to play."

"Play, my eyeball," said Lizzie.

She pulled a tattered pajama top from the box and raced to cover the next window.

8
Michigan

First, Pickwick.

Now, Uncle Frank.

No, Mom didn't dump Uncle Frank in the washer for a bath. But Uncle Frank is going away.

Another sad good-bye.

Mom says it's just for a few months. Grandpop Jacobs in Michigan broke his leg. He needs help, especially since he's moving from his house to an apartment. He can't do all that packing and unpacking alone.

Mom can't go. She has me to take care of.

Uncle Frank isn't married. He doesn't have any kids. It will be easier for him.

"What about our star party?" I sniffled.

Uncle Frank patted my hand. "When I come back, I promise."

"Maybe you won't come back," I said. "Maybe you'll like it out there in Michigan."

"I do like Michigan," he said. "It's where your mom and I grew up. But I like it better here."

"How come?"

Uncle Frank gave me a hug. "Because you're here, short-stuff."

• • •

The day before Uncle Frank was to leave, he came over with a package. It was a box of stars. All afternoon he and I put them up in my room. Across the ceiling. Halfway down the walls. We put them in the shapes of constellations. Orion the Hunter. Taurus the Bull. The Big Dipper. The Little Dog.

When it got dark that night they shimmered, just like real stars.

• • •

The next morning Lizzie's folks gave Uncle Frank a going-away brunch.

Sam made his famous pancakes. There

were scrambled eggs and bacon and ham. There were fruit salad and apple muffins. And for Lizzie's mom, a tray of beef sticks.

The entire neighborhood came over to say good-bye.

Granny Fryola promised Uncle Frank a free crabcake sandwich when he came back.

Mr. and Mrs. Bitterman gave Uncle Frank a stack of magazines for the long bus ride.

I gave him a key chain. It had a rainbow with the words I LOVE YOU printed across it.

Lizzie gave him a picture of herself and Charley.

The Woolery twins gave him a finger painting. "It's an elephant," Mrs. Woolery explained.

Betsy and Bootsie climbed up Uncle Frank's legs. "Don't go away!" they pleaded.

Lizzie glowered at the twins. "Dorky little spies," she hissed.

I couldn't believe her. "Lizzie, they're only three years old."

"So was the alligator that bit off that guy's thumb at Gator-Haven."

9
Garfish and Cigar Sharks

There was one good thing about being Lizzie's manager for The Little Miss Seafood Pageant: It kept my mind off Uncle Frank. I really missed him.

"So, what's your talent gonna be?" I asked Lizzie one day.

We were in her room. Charley was snoozing on the beanbag chair.

"I'm going to sing," she said.

"I didn't know you could sing."

Lizzie clamped her hands on her hips. "Any turkey can sing."

"Do you know a fish song?" I said. "It's gotta be about a fish."

Lizzie gave me a smug look. "I know 'Ten Little Fishies.'"

Everybody knew "Ten Little Fishies." From kindergarten. I asked Lizzie to sing it for me.

"Why?" she sniffed. "Don't you believe I can sing?"

"Sure I believe it. It's just that I'm your manager, so I think I should hear for myself."

Lizzie rolled her eyes. "Oh, all right." She began. "Ten little fishies swimming in a bog..."

She sounded like a woodpecker caught in a rainspout. Even Charley seemed to twitch at the high notes.

"One met up with an old bullfrog..."

I stuck my fingers in my ears. "Stoooooop!"

Lizzie stopped singing. "What's the matter?"

I gave her a crooked smile. "How's your dancing?"

• • •

If this was The Little Miss Quack Contest, Lizzie's dancing would have been perfect. She waddled around the room like a duck, feet clopping, arms flapping like wings.

I shook my head. "Sorry."

Lizzie threw one of her pillows at me. "Hey! You're my manager. You're supposed to encourage me."

"I will," I told her. "Once we find something you can do."

Lizzie flopped backwards onto her bed. She began naming her true talents: "I can catch flies with my bare hands. I can cure warts. I can eat eleven pancakes at one sitting. I can thread a fat juicy night crawler on a fishhook without throwing up. Hey!" she exclaimed. "*That's* a fish thing."

"No way," I said. "Maybe you won't throw up, but the audience will."

"Okay, Miss Smarty-Pants, you're the manager. You come up with an idea."

Which is exactly what I did. The *perfect* idea for Lizzie Logan, smartest kid in the universe.

I said, "Recite what you know about fish."

"Huh?"

"Oh, not the usual stuff. The strange stuff. Like when you told me about it raining frogs in Russia. Miss Kelsey really liked that."

Lizzie was silent for five minutes. She paced back and forth. She looked out the window. She looked at the bed. She looked at Charley. Finally she looked at me. She pointed her finger between my eyes. She nodded. "You're right."

Lizzie Logan seldom accused anyone but herself of being right. I tried to stay cool, but inside I was shouting, *whoopee!*

"I know plenty about fish," she said. She began spouting fish facts: "Sea horse *fathers* give birth to the babies . . . a garfish has green bones . . . there's a shark you can carry in your pocket . . ."

I gaped at her. "No way."

Lizzie smirked. "Absolutely. Sharks come in all sizes. A cigar shark would fit in your pocket."

A cigar shark. Wow! I'd never even heard of such a creature. I patted Lizzie on the back. "Way to go, girl."

For the first time since Lizzie had entered The Little Miss Seafood Pageant, I thought she just might win.

10
Baby-Sitting the Woolery Twins

Mrs. Woolery had just broken her toe. She had to go to the doctor. My mother offered to baby-sit the Woolery twins, so they were coming over to our place for the afternoon.

I was about to go over to Lizzie's. This was the day Lizzie was going to practice her pageant smile. She had tried out quite a few during the week. Big, toothy grin. Lips shut tight. Lips opened a crack. A giggly smile. A shy kind of smile.

I voted for the shy kind of smile.

Lizzie preferred the big, toothy grin.

Big, toothy grin it was.

Mom said Lizzie would have to do her

smiling at our house. "I need you to help with Betsy and Bootsie."

I understood. The Woolery twins could be a handful.

"Okay," I told her. "But Lizzie's not gonna be happy."

I was right.

"Christopher jumping catfish!" Lizzie screeched into the phone. "I can't practice my smile in front of those two little spy-niks."

"Come on," I said. "You can't really believe the Woolery twins are spies."

"I can and I do," declared Lizzie.

"Okay," I said. "I'll come over to your place after Mrs. Woolery takes the twins back."

I hung up.

"What's a spy?"

I jumped a mile. It was Betsy, scrunched behind the chair where I'd been sitting.

Bootsie was scrunched up next to her. She piped, "A spy is bad."

"Bad?" said Betsy.

"Yeah," said Bootsie. "Spies shoot people."

She pointed her finger at me. "BANG!"

Betsy joined in. "BANG! BANG!"

"Stop that!" I said.

"BANG! BANG! BANG!"

Mom came into the room. "What's all the racket?"

"I'm getting a headache," I said.

"We're playing spies," said Betsy.

Bootsie jumped up and down. "Spies shot our mommy's toe off."

Mom laughed. "No. Your mommy bumped her toe on her sewing table."

"Spies did it," Bootsie squealed.

"Spies," said Betsy.

Mom sighed. "Milk and cookie time."

We followed her into the kitchen. Mom set out a plate of oatmeal cookies. I poured the milk.

A few minutes later, Dad walked in the back door. "Hi, small fries." He tousled the twins' hair.

Bootsie turned around in her chair. She aimed her finger at Dad's belly. "BANG!"

Dad staggered backward. He groaned.

"Ya got me, cowpoke."

"She's not a cowpoke," I said.

Dad reached for a cookie. "No?"

"She's a spy," said Betsy.

"A big, bad spy," said Bootsie.

I got up to rinse my glass. "Better not let Lizzie Logan hear you say that," I told them.

11
Marigold Seeds

Lizzie didn't go to school the next day. Mom said Lizzie and her folks had something important to do.

I asked what it was. All Mom would say was that I'd find out later. Grown-ups—yeesh!

I wondered if Lizzie's absence had anything to do with the baby. Were Lizzie and her folks shopping for a playpen? Or a high chair? Or a stroller?

Probably not. Shopping didn't count as an excuse for missing school. The principal, Mr. Gates, would be on the phone in five minutes. The truant officer would be banging at Lizzie's door. Besides, Lizzie still didn't like the idea of a little brother or sister.

She'd rather take a zillion math tests than shop for baby stuff.

I walked to school by myself.

When I got there, Miss Kelsey had starter trays set up on the folding table. Our class was going to plant marigold seeds. I planted five of them. If all five bloomed I'd give one to Mom, one to Dad, one to Uncle Frank (when he came back from Michigan), one to Lizzie, and one to myself.

I remembered seeing a gardening show on public television. It was about a woman who did an experiment in her own kitchen. She planted seeds in pots. She set the pots on sunny windowsills. She tended them. She watered them. Each got the same amount of care—except that the woman prayed for some of the seeds. And guess what? Those were the seeds that did best.

I figured I'd try it. I said a little prayer for my five marigold seeds. Then I felt guilty. It didn't seem right to pray for just my own seeds. So I said another prayer for all the seeds in the third grade.

I could just hear Lizzie: *What! You prayed for Kayleen Bitterman's marigold seeds?*

I had to laugh.

We cleaned up the potting soil and puddles of water. We had spelling. Then reading. Then lunch.

All day I wondered about Lizzie and her folks. I wondered what their "something important to do" was about.

When I got home from school that afternoon, Lizzie was waiting on my front porch. She was sitting in the old rocking chair, creaking back and forth. She had a goofy expression on her face. "Well, pal," she said, "say good-bye to Lizzie Logan."

My heart sank. Good-bye. Now I knew why she hadn't come to school. Now I knew what the important thing was about.

It was about moving.

With the baby due in August, Lizzie's folks probably wanted a new house. Something bigger. More yard. Less traffic. Far, far from Mole Street.

12
No More Lizzie Logan

I was wrong.

"Moving?" Lizzie laughed out loud. "Don't be a peanut head. You think I'd move away from my best friend? Huh?"

I shrugged and turned away. I didn't want her to see my eyes misting up.

Lizzie twirled me around the porch. "You're stuck with me forever!"

When she stopped, I glared at her. "So why did you say 'good-bye to Lizzie Logan'?"

"Because Lizzie Logan is outta here. From now on"—she stepped back, she took a bow—"call me, tah-dah, Lizzie Logan Bright."

I screeched and jumped up and down. "You mean it? All the legal stuff's done?"

46

Lizzie beamed. "Yep. I am Sam Wesley Bright's daughter. It's official!"

It was my turn to twirl Lizzie. We laughed and shrieked and twirled so much, we nearly fell over the porch railing.

"And you know the best thing?" Lizzie said when we had flopped out of breath onto the rocking chairs.

"No, what?"

"He whistled!"

"Huh?"

"Dad—when all the papers were signed—he whistled!"

I couldn't help it. I hugged her right there and bawled like a baby. I was so happy for her.

• • •

It was a great night on Mole Street.

Sam cooked up a feast. All Lizzie's favorite foods: spaghetti with mushrooms, pickles, tuna salad, pancakes, peanut butter fudge, vanilla ice cream, chocolate layer cake.

Everyone came. Even Kayleen Bitterman. She brought Lizzie a pair of pink socks.

Lizzie doesn't like pink stuff. I figured Lizzie would pinch Kayleen's nose or something, but she didn't. She simply said, "Aren't they pretty," all nice and polite.

Joey Fryola told Lizzie she was welcome to borrow his ant farm anytime she wanted.

Mom got Lizzie a poster of two whales breaching. "See, they're happy for you, too," Mom said, kissing Lizzie's cheek.

I gave Lizzie my book about bats—to keep.

When the Woolerys came, I expected Lizzie to march Betsy and Bootsie right out the front door. Instead, she gave them each a hug.

I gaped at her. She gave me a goofy smile. "Tonight I love everybody—even the little spy-niks."

While the party was going on, Uncle Frank phoned. He had gotten the news all the way in Michigan. He wanted to say congratulations, too.

"I miss you," I told him when it was my turn to talk.

"I miss you, too, short-stuff."

After dessert Sam brought out a big box. It was wrapped in shiny silver paper. He set it in front of Lizzie.

"Better keep that paper away from Bootsie," said Dad.

Bootsie likes shiny things. Once she grabbed a ring right off Lizzie's finger and swallowed it.

When Lizzie opened the box, her eyes popped like a frog's. "A telescope!" she squealed.

Sam smoothed Lizzie's hair. "I hope the wait wasn't too hard, old girl."

Over dessert I said to Lizzie, "You got your telescope. Now you don't have to be in that dumb Little Miss Seafood Pageant."

Lizzie didn't seem to hear me. She stuffed a piece of fudge in her mouth and went, "Mmmmmmmm."

At nine o'clock Lizzie's mom made an announcement. "Music time!"

She put a tape in the tape player. The song playing was "Daddy's Little Girl."

Sam pulled Lizzie to her feet and into his arms. While the rest of us stood around them in a circle, Lizzie Bright danced with her dad.

The grown-ups had tears in their eyes. Lizzie's mom pulled a tissue from her pocket and blew her nose.

Then Bootsie and Betsy Woolery elbowed their way into the center of the circle. They began to dance. They leaped like little tadpoles. They swayed. They spun. They bumped butts.

Charley got into the act, too. He chased Bootsie into a lamp.

Everyone broke up.

I was sure Uncle Frank could hear our laughter all the way in Michigan.

13
Good-bye, Winter

March twenty-first was the first day of spring.

In class our marigold seeds were sprouting. *All* of them.

Miss Kelsey had taken down the cotton-ball snowmen that decorated the walls. We put them away in boxes.

She erased winter words like "snowmobile," "arctic," "sleigh," and "reindeer" from the back blackboard.

She wrote in bright yellow chalk: "Good-bye, winter!"

But it didn't feel like good-bye, winter.

It was gray and damp and cold. I had forgotten my mittens, so instead of going out to recess, I stayed in to hang cardboard robins around the room.

After school Lizzie lent me one of her gloves. We each kept our bare hand in a pocket.

"Wanna help me finish my octopus costume?" Lizzie asked.

"Finish it?" I said. "Why? You got your telescope. You don't need the prize money now."

Lizzie was quiet for a minute. Then she said, "I'm still gonna enter The Little Miss Seafood Pageant."

"If you don't need the prize money, why do you still care about being Little Miss Seafood?"

"I don't care."

"Then why bother?"

She looked away from me. "Because—" She blinked. She cleared her throat. "—I want to do something that will make Dad proud of me. And Mom." Her voice was whispery. "You may not know this, Heather, but sometimes I can be a real pain in the eyeball."

Oh, I knew it.

"You really think being Little Miss Seafood

will make them proud?" I said.

"Yeah."

"But what if you don't win?"

Lizzie poked me with her elbow. "Don't even think that. I *gotta* win."

• • •

Lizzie's dad had attached eight frayed vacuum cleaner hoses to an old flannel robe. Lizzie's mom had gotten her a gray ski mask.

"How do I look?" Lizzie, the octopus, asked me as she clink-clunked around her bedroom.

"Terrific!" I told her. "So what's to finish?"

"It needs more color," she said. "I was thinking we could add some seaweed."

Lizzie got scissors and green construction paper. She cut the green paper into strips. I glued the strips into a long paper chain. Charley snatched the paper chain and whisked it away. We made another one.

Lizzie looped the chain around her vacuum cleaner arms. Then she stood in front of her mirror.

She admired herself from the front.

She admired herself from the side.

She craned her neck so she could admire herself from the back. She whooped, "Let Little Miss Bitterman top this baby!"

• • •

That night I said my usual prayers, which of course included the third-grade marigolds.

Then I said a prayer that Lizzie would be crowned Little Miss Seafood so her mom and dad would be proud of her and not think of her as a pain in the eyeball.

Then I lay looking at the stars that spattered my ceiling and walls. The stars that Uncle Frank had given me.

Each constellation glowed brightly. Orion the Hunter. Taurus the Bull. Big Dipper. Little Dog.

I drifted off to sleep dreaming that Uncle Frank was back. We were at a star party at Valley Forge Park. Stargazing. Together.

14
Second Banana

Lizzie was in the backyard. Hole digging.

"Now what?" I asked.

She gave me a look. "It's a boy," she growled.

I nearly fainted. "Your mom had the baby!"

"No." She flung a shovelful of dirt. "She had a test."

I scratched my head. "A test can tell you the baby's a boy?"

Lizzie snapped. "Don't you know anything about modern medicine?"

"Not as much as you, I guess."

That seemed to please Lizzie.

"So, it's a boy," I said. "What's so bad about that?"

"What's bad about that, noodlehead, is

that I'm gonna be second banana now."

"Second banana?"

"Yeah. Fathers have a thing about sons."

"They do?"

"They like them better than daughters."

"Says who?"

"Says culture! Says society!" Lizzie poked the air with her shovel. "Says public television!"

"Public television?"

"Uh-huh. A month ago I saw this program about some ancient tribe. They left their baby girls in the woods to die. The fathers wanted sons."

I patted Lizzie's back. "I don't think Sam's gonna leave you in the woods," I told her. "Besides, you're no baby. If Sam did stick you in the woods, all you'd have to do is walk right out. You could come to my house."

Lizzie smacked her forehead. "You are such a turkey. I know Dad's not gonna stick me in the woods."

"So what are you worrying about?"

"He's gonna want to spend more time with his son, that's what. Fishing . . . hiking . . . football games . . ."

"Sam took *you* fishing," I reminded her.

"That's because there weren't any little boys around."

More dirt went flying.

• • •

At supper I asked my dad, "Do you like boys better than girls?"

Dad looked at Mom and me. He smiled. "I can't imagine liking anybody more than I like my girls."

"But suppose you had a son?"

"I'd like him, too."

I popped a French fry into my mouth. "Would you take him fishing?"

"I don't go fishing."

"Sam's baby is gonna be a boy. I guess he'll take him fishing."

Mom raised her eyebrows. "So that's what this is about? Lizzie found out she's going to have a brother."

I nodded. "She thinks she's gonna be

second banana now."

Mom sighed. "Poor Lizzie."

Dad served himself another piece of chicken. "Poor Sam."

15
Almost April

March is nearly over, and I'm looking forward to April, which will be a special month. First there's the Little Miss Seafood Pageant on April eighteenth.

Lizzie and I often walk past the old Bagel Box, which is now Granny Fryola's Fish Store. Granny is usually there—sweeping floors, washing windows, polishing the doorknob.

Lizzie makes sure to flash Granny the big, toothy grin.

We spend a lot of time at the library. Lizzie and I look up more weird facts about fish. She has a collection of seventy-eight facts now and wants to recite them all for the pageant.

As Lizzie's manager, I felt I had to tell her that seventy-eight fish facts would put everyone to sleep.

For once, she didn't argue. She said she would recite only fifty. I told her she'd better talk fast.

Also in April is my birthday. On the twenty-first I'll be nine years old. I haven't decided yet what I want from my parents.

Lizzie says to ask for an ant farm. That's because she wants an ant farm.

I'm not into ants. So I'm thinking I won't *ask* for anything. Maybe I'll let Mom and Dad surprise me. I like surprises.

Lizzie says surprises can be dangerous.

"How?" I asked.

"Once some lady's husband bought her a boa constrictor for her birthday. He put it in her bed with a big red bow around its neck."

"What happened?"

"You don't want to know!"

"I don't think Mom and Dad would ever surprise me with a boa constrictor."

"Maybe not," said Lizzie. "But, anyway—enough about your birthday. There're more important things to think about."

16
No Turning Back

It was the night of the Little Miss Seafood Pageant.

Lizzie paced in her room. Her octopus arms clink-clunked. Her big, toothy grin seemed lopsided.

"Stop being so nervous," I told her. "You'll do fine."

Lizzie's eyes sparked. "I don't want to do fine. I want to win."

Lizzie's dad came in. "You gals ready?"

Lizzie took a deep breath. "Let's get this show on the road."

Two seconds later she was in the bathroom throwing up.

Lizzie's mom pressed a cool washcloth to Lizzie's forehead. "Maybe you should just stay home."

Lizzie sat on the edge of the tub. "No way. I'm going."

I patted her arm. Her *real* arm.

Charley licked Lizzie's hand.

Sam brought her a cup of peppermint tea. "Sip this, old girl. It'll make you feel better."

After a few minutes, Lizzie stood up. She flung the green paper chain over her shoulder. "Okay, let's do it."

Lizzie's mom shook her head. "I don't know . . ."

Sam put his arm around Lizzie. "We can turn back anytime."

With her head held high, Lizzie marched into the hall. "That won't be necessary," she said all grown-up like.

Lizzie's mom said, "Well, then, break a leg."

Lizzie turned. "Huh?"

"It's a show biz saying. It means good luck."

"Break a tentacle," said Sam.

• • •

It was crowded at Granny Fryola's Fish Store.

There must have been fifty folding chairs set up.

Mr. Fryola had built a small stage out of plywood and boards. Mrs. Fryola had decorated it with blue plastic fish.

Joey Fryola directed Lizzie to the back room.

Lizzie pointed at me. "She comes, too. She's my manager."

"No managers," said Joey. "Contestants only."

I gave Lizzie a hug, which wasn't easy with all those dangly arms. "Good luck," I whispered.

I took a seat next to Mom.

People were laughing and talking. Kayleen Bitterman's father was setting up his video camera. Sue-Ann LeBoon's little cousin Ralph was chasing Betsy Woolery with a rubber roach. Bootsie Woolery had climbed up a dried codfish display. Her father was trying to coax her down.

She bonked him on the head with a codfish.

Then the lights flicked off and on, and Granny Fryola stepped out onto the stage.

Kayleen's dad started his camera rolling.

Mrs. LeBoon pulled her nephew onto her lap.

Betsy Woolery sat down next to Sam.

Bootsie Woolery, still perched atop the codfish boxes, started clapping.

The Little Miss Seafood Pageant was about to begin.

17
Five Contestants

Sue-Ann LeBoon was the first contestant to be introduced.

She was dressed like a fisherman—plaid shirt, straw hat, fishing pole.

Her cousin, Ralph, called out: "Catch me a fishie, Sue-Ann!"

"Hush!" said Mrs. LeBoon.

Sue-Ann smiled at the audience. Nothing special, just her usual smile.

The she started to sing "Gone Fishin'." Sue-Ann has a pretty good voice. But she didn't just stand there singing. She acted the song out.

The audience liked it. She got a lot of applause.

Next was Erica Chapko.

Erica takes dancing lessons, so I wasn't

surprised when she tapped across the stage in shiny black shoes. She wore a denim dress with a crab painted on the skirt.

So far, so good.

But Erica must have been concentrating too hard on her dance steps, because she forgot to smile.

Everyone clapped anyway.

A first grader waving a goldfish puppet came out after Erica. She told a goldfish joke. It wasn't funny. Still, everyone laughed politely.

Then came Lizzie, clink-clunking onto the stage.

I could tell she wasn't nervous anymore.

She bowed. She waved. She flashed the biggest, toothiest grin ever.

She recited one fish fact after another:

"Minnows have teeth in their throat . . . the marine catfish can taste with any part of its body . . . the head of the lantern fish glows . . ."

On and on and on she went until she was out of breath.

Finally—and this was something she must have decided to do at the last minute—Lizzie took off her paper chain seaweed and draped it around Granny Fryola.

People in the crowd whistled.

I gave Lizzie two thumbs up.

Bootsie Woolery scooted down from the codfish. She ran onstage to give Lizzie a hug.

Sam beamed. Mrs. Bright wiped a tear from her eye.

And then Granny Fryola announced the final contestant. Kayleen Bitterman.

Kayleen floated onstage.

By floated I don't mean walked gracefully. Kayleen wasn't walking at all. She was reclining. On a float. A float that was decorated to look like the sea.

She was a mermaid.

Kayleen's father must have worked oodles of overtime to pay for all the jewels and sequins on Kayleen's costume.

She shimmered green or silver, depending on how the light hit her sparkly scales.

Even her smile glittered.

There were real pink flowers in her hair and around her neck.

She recited a poem about a mermaid in a voice I had never heard coming out of Kayleen's mouth. Not a whine in it—all soft and sweet as cotton candy.

When Kayleen finished the poem, a small fountain erupted on the far side of the float.

The audience cheered.

I glanced over at Granny Fryola.

She looked as though she had just seen the eighth wonder of the world.

18
And the Winner Is

No one was surprised when Granny Fryola announced the winner. "Let's hear it for Kayleen Bitterman . . . Little Miss Seafood!"

Once again Kayleen floated onstage.

Granny set a crown of clamshells on Kayleen's head. Kayleen's mother swooned in her seat. Kayleen's father videotaped the swoon, then turned the camera on his daughter.

People gathered around Kayleen.

"Congratulations!"

"Way to go!"

"Super job!"

Betsy Woolery climbed onto Kayleen's float. Bootsie plucked a sequin from Kayleen's tail and tried to eat it. Mrs. LeBoon caught her just in time.

At last, Granny waved her arms at the crowd. "Quiet, please!" she yelled.

Everyone settled down.

Granny said, "Let's bring out the other contestants and give them a big round of applause."

Sue-Ann LeBoon, Erica Chapko, and the first grader came out. Granny handed each girl a certificate for a free clam roll.

I looked at Mom. "Where's Lizzie?"

Mom shrugged. The she leaned across to Sam. "Where's Lizzie?"

Sam stood up. He called out for Lizzie.

Betsy Woolery joined him. "Lizzie!"

"Where's Lizzie octopus?" Bootsie Woolery shouted.

Granny Fryola sent Joey into the back room.

We heard a clink-clunking—Lizzie's vacuum cleaner arms.

Joey came out. He was carrying Lizzie's costume.

Lizzie wasn't in it.

19
Worried

Lizzie's mother checked the fish store bathroom. Sam and Dad checked the basement.

No Lizzie.

Mr. Woolery checked the back alley. Mr. LeBoon checked the deli next door.

No Lizzie.

Granny patted Lizzie's mom on the shoulder. "Maybe she went home."

Sam drove back to Mole Street.

We looked all through the house. Even in closets, under beds.

No Lizzie.

I suggested the backyard. "Lizzie might be digging one of her holes."

Sam got a flashlight from the kitchen. We followed as he checked every corner of the yard. Lizzie wasn't there. Neither were any new holes.

Next, we went to our house. Mudroom. Bedrooms. Coal bin.

No Lizzie anywhere.

Sam tried not to look worried, but he did a rotten job.

Lizzie's mother started to cry. "Lizzie wasn't feeling well tonight. We should have kept her home."

My mother said, "I'll make some tea."

Just then the phone rang. It was Mrs. Woolery asking about Lizzie.

"We haven't found her yet," Dad whispered.

Mrs. Woolery offered to keep me at her place so Mom and Dad could keep searching for Lizzie.

"I don't want to go to the Woolerys'," I protested. "I want to help."

Dad handed me my jacket. "You can help best now by doing what I ask."

Kayleen Bitterman was at the Woolerys', too. So were Joey Fryola, Sue-Ann LeBoon, and her cousin Ralph. And, of course, Betsy and Bootsie.

The minute I walked in, Kayleen sniffed. "I hope you aren't blaming me that Lizzie's gone."

I didn't answer. I sat on the sofa next to Ralph. He was sound asleep and snoring.

Kayleen plucked a speck of lint from her frilly pink bathrobe. "I can't help it I got voted Little Miss Seafood."

Mrs. Woolery set a tray of crackers and juice on the coffee table. "Nobody's blaming you, Kayleen."

Sue-Ann shivered. "Maybe somebody kidnapped Lizzie."

"Spies did it!" cried Bootsie, stuffing a cracker into her mouth.

"Spies shot Lizzie's toe off!" piped Betsy.

"Nobody's been kidnapped," said Mrs. Woolery. "And no one's toe was shot off."

Joey Fryola poured himself a glass of juice. "Lizzie might have gone to my place. To visit my ant farm."

Mrs. Woolery nodded. "I'm sure the

police will check."

"Police!" I screeched. Sue-Ann's cousin bolted awake. "Why call the police?"

Mrs. Woolery sat on the arm of the sofa. She brushed a wisp of my hair back. "Heather, honey, the police are skilled at finding people."

I looked out the front window. It was really dark. The moon was like a toenail clipping.

I thought about my best friend, Lizzie. Sad. Scared. Alone in the night. Maybe even in danger.

I burst into tears.

• • •

It was about 9:45 when Mr. Woolery brought out the sleeping bags. One for Kayleen. One for Sue-Ann. One for Joey.

Sue-Ann's cousin had fallen asleep again on the sofa. Mrs. Woolery covered him with an afghan.

"Heather, you can sleep in Bootsie's bed. Bootsie will sleep with Betsy tonight."

"Any news?" I asked.

Mrs. Woolery let out a long breath and shook her head. "Not a word."

Betsy and Bootsie got into their pajamas.

Then Betsy went to the bookshelf. She chose a book and brought it to me. It was *Stellaluna*. "Read me a story."

Bootsie grabbed the book. "Mine!"

Betsy wailed. "Mommy says share!"

Bootsie shrieked. "You got your own books!"

Mrs. Woolery rushed into the bedroom. "Stop it this instant!" she scolded. "This is no night for nonsense."

"Bootsie won't share." Betsy sniffled.

"Bed," said Mrs. Woolery. "Now!"

The twins climbed into Betsy's bed.

Bootsie squirmed. "Betsy won't move over."

Betsy pouted. "Bootsie's hogging all the room."

Mrs. Woolery held her ears. "That does it! I'm calling Daddy."

Suddenly the twins were silent.

Betsy fell asleep.

Bootsie lay there making hand shadows on the wall.

I put on an old T-shirt of Mrs. Woolery's for a nightie. I got into bed. I closed my eyes. I started to say my usual prayers, but all I could think of was Lizzie. *Please let them find her. Please let her be all right.*

Something ponked me on the head.

I opened my eyes. It was a tiny stuffed rabbit. Bootsie had thrown it across the room.

"You can sleep with Puff-bunny," she said.

I smiled. "Thanks, Bootsie."

"I miss Lizzie," said Bootsie.

"Me, too," I whispered.

20
Here's What Happened

"Did you *really* miss me?"

Lizzie was sitting up in bed eating chocolate chip pancakes. It was the morning after the pageant.

"Yes, I missed you," I told her. "But mostly I was worried. You didn't even say good-bye."

Lizzie winced. "I know. I feel awful."

I pointed to the egg-sized lump on her head. To the scrapes and bruises on her arms. "You *look* awful."

She looked in the mirror. "Don't remind me." She mopped a piece of pancake in syrup and ate it. "You know the real reason why I entered the contest, don't you?"

"Sure," I said. "So your new dad would be proud of you."

"And to make him like me as much as the new baby."

"Right."

"So what happens?" said Lizzie. "I lose, that's what." She stabbed at a pancake with her fork. "I couldn't even win a silly fish crown from tooty-snooty Kayleen Bitterman."

"So?" I said.

"So?" she said. "If I couldn't compete with Kayleen Bitterman how could I ever compete with an adorable brand-new baby boy?"

"That's dumb," I told her. "You don't have to compete with anybody. Sam has enough love for you and a whole herd of baby boys."

"You think?" she said.

"I know," I said. "You should have seen him last night. He was worried sick about you."

"Really?"

"Really. And besides, who do you think made you those pancakes you're eating?"

She nodded and took another bite.

"And double besides—dads love their girl kids as much as their boy kids."

She looked at me. "That so?"

"Absolutely," I said. "My own dad told me."

Lizzie chewed some more and nodded. "I guess I know all that now. But I didn't then. I wasn't thinking. I was just feeling . . ."

"Rotten is what you were feeling, right?"

"Right," she said.

Then Lizzie told me what happened.

When Granny Fryola announced Kayleen as the winner, Lizzie got out of her costume quick and snuck out the back door. She figured she'd run away.

Lizzie ran about four blocks when suddenly she didn't know where she was running to. She needed to think, but not at home.

Right away she thought of The Good Old Days. The shed. Our old play place.

"I knew I could get in," she said, "because—"

I piped up. "Because we were the ones who lost the padlock."

"Right," she said.

By then Lizzie was too tired to think. All she wanted to do was sleep. She squeezed under that old desk. Too uncomfortable. She climbed on top of an old wooden barrel. That was worse. Then she tried that crummy old wicker chair that hangs from a hook on the wall. She stood on the barrel and climbed into it, squirming around trying to get comfortable. That's when she fell. Next thing she knew the policeman had found her.

"Right," I said. I giggled. "I heard the policeman found you on a pile of old baskets, knocked cuckoo. He said you looked at him all goofy and asked: "Am I in Michigan?"

21
Hello

I woke up on April twenty-first, my birthday, to a familiar face.

"Uncle Frank!" I squealed. I leaped into his arms.

"Couldn't miss your birthday, short-stuff."

He carried me piggyback down the stairs and into the kitchen. There were nine red balloons tied to my chair.

"Eggs?" Mom asked. "French toast? Cornflakes? Your wish is my command."

"Donuts?" said Dad. "I'll run down to O'Dell's Donut Shop. Chocolate glazed? Cream? Jelly?"

"Did I hear somebody say donuts?"

It was Lizzie. She was carrying a purple bag with HAPPY BIRTHDAY written on it in big yellow letters.

She set it on the table in front of me. I lifted the sheet of tissue paper. Grinning up at me—*big toothy* grin—was a fuzzy green alligator. "It's not Pickwick," Lizzie said. "But I hope you like him."

I pulled the alligator out of the bag by his snout. I gave him a hug. "I do."

"What'll you call him?" Lizzie asked.

I thought for a minute. Then I giggled. "Noodlenose!"

Dad tweaked Mom's cheek. He turned to me. "Better warn Noodlenose to stay out of the laundry room."

I decided on donuts for my birthday breakfast. We'd all go down to O'Dell's and eat our donuts right in the shop.

I got dressed and ready to go.

Outside, the sky was as blue as a crayon. The air smelled sweet. A sparrow flew to the tree in our front yard. "Hello, bird," I called.

Lately there had been too many goodbyes. Good-bye to Pickwick. Good-bye to Uncle Frank. Good-bye to winter. Almost good-bye to Lizzie Logan Bright.

But today was all hellos. Hello to being nine. Hello to Uncle Frank. Hello to balloons and surprises to come. Hello Noodlenose. I couldn't get enough of hellos.

I grabbed Lizzie's hand and spun her around right in the middle of Mole Street. "Hello, Lizzie!"

She pulled me to a stop. "You know," she said, "in four months I'll be saying a pretty big hello myself."

"Right," I said. "Hello, baby."

"Yeah," said Lizzie. She smiled. She looked off up the street as if she could actually see August coming. "Hello, little brother."

Lizzie Logan

will make you laugh!

Read all three books:

Lizzie Logan Wears Purple Sunglasses 0-689-81848-3
$3.99 / $5.50 Canadian

Lizzie Logan Gets Married 0-689-82071-2
$3.99 / $5.50 Canadian

Lizzie Logan, Second Banana 0-689-83048-3
$3.99 / $5.50 Canadian

Simon & Schuster Children's Publishing
www.SimonSaysKids.com